GREETINGS FROM SOMEWHERE

SOMEWHERE

The Mystery of the Icy Paw Prints

BY HARPER PARIS • ILLUSTRATED BY MARCOS CALO

LITTLE SIMON

New York   London   Toronto   Sydney   New Delhi

This book is a work of fiction. Any references to historical events, real people, or real places are used fictitiously. Other names, characters, places, and events are products of the author's imagination, and any resemblance to actual events or places or persons, living or dead, is entirely coincidental.

 LITTLE SIMON

An imprint of Simon & Schuster Children's Publishing Division · 1230 Avenue of the Americas, New York, New York 10020 · First Little Simon paperback edition October 2015 · Copyright © 2015 by Simon & Schuster, Inc. All rights reserved, including the right of reproduction in whole or in part in any form. LITTLE SIMON is a registered trademark of Simon & Schuster, Inc., and associated colophon is a trademark of Simon & Schuster, Inc. For information about special discounts for bulk purchases, please contact Simon & Schuster Special Sales at 1-866-506-1949 or business@simonandschuster.com. The Simon & Schuster Speakers Bureau can bring authors to your live event. For more information or to book an event contact the Simon & Schuster Speakers Bureau at 1-866-248-3049 or visit our website at www.simonspeakers.com. Designed by John Daly. The text of this book was set in ITC Stone Informal. Manufactured in the United States of America 0915 FFG 10 9 8 7 6 5 4 3 2 1 Cataloging-in-Publication Data for this title is available from the Library of Congress.
ISBN 978-1-4814-2374-8 (hc)
ISBN 978-1-4814-2373-1 (pbk)
ISBN 978-1-4814-2375-5 (eBook)

TABLE OF CONTENTS

CHAPTER 1

Flightseeing!

"We're going to crash into the mountain!" Ethan Briar cried out.

"That's not a mountain, silly. That's a cloud," his twin sister, Ella, said with a laugh.

Their pilot, Zane, steered their small plane through a thick cloud. For a moment the whole world was white.

Then they reached the other side,

and the snowy face of Mount McKinley rose into the sky. Even from a distance, it looked massive!

"Now, *that's* a mountain," their father, Andrew, said. "Isn't that incredible, kids? It's the tallest one in North America!"

Their mother, Josephine, held her camera up to the window and clicked.

"This is quite the view. My readers are going to love these photos!"

Mrs. Briar worked as a travel writer for their hometown newspaper, the *Brookeston Times*. The Briars were traveling around the world so she could write articles about different places.

Alaska was the eighth place they had visited so far. It was very different from their last stop, which was Australia. In Australia, the twins had gone snorkeling in the warm waters of the Coral Sea. Here in Alaska, it was winter, and there was snow everywhere.

Zane circled Mount McKinley several times before nosing the plane

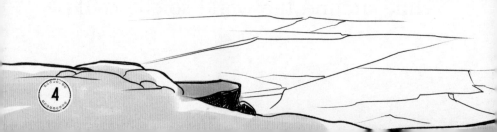

down to a nearby lake. He coasted just above the frozen surface. "There's a moose on the shore!" he said, pointing.

The twins craned their necks. An enormous moose gnawed on the bark of a tree.

After Mount McKinley, they headed south. They flew over volcanoes,

icefalls, and glaciers. This was the twins' first flightseeing experience, which was sightseeing from the air. It was pretty amazing!

They soon reached Prince William Sound. A dozen seals sunned themselves on a large sheet of floating ice. Ella gazed out the window. "I can't believe we're in the same country as Brookeston," she said in awe.

Ethan gasped. "Good idea, Ella!"

"What's a good idea?" Ella asked, confused.

Ethan leaned forward in his seat. "Mom, Dad, can we go home for a few days? This is the first time we've been back in the United States in so long!"

"Oh! And we could see Grandpa Harry and all our friends!" Ella gushed.

"I'm really sorry, guys. Just because we're in the United States again doesn't mean we're close to home," Mrs. Briar replied.

"Brookeston is about four thousand miles from here," Mr. Briar added.

Four thousand miles?

The twins turned to each other with heavy sighs. They had been traveling for what seemed like forever. They really missed home.

Alaska wasn't a foreign country— but it sure felt like it was!

CHAPTER 2
Homesick

That night, the Briars returned to their hotel in the city of Anchorage. Ethan and Ella found two e-mails waiting for them.

The first one was from Theo, who was Ethan's best friend. Ethan missed Theo. He missed building top-secret forts and doing crazy science experiments with things they found.

Hey, Ethan!

Guess what? We have a new pet in our class! He's a gerbil, and his name is Speedy. His favorite treats are popcorn and cheese! Thanks for the post-card from Australia. The picture of the coral reef looked supercool. What country are you in now? Will you be home by soccer season?

Goal!

Theo

Ethan frowned. He had no idea if they would be home by soccer season. Probably not. He thought about Mrs. Applebaum's classroom at

Brookeston Elementary School. He tried to imagine where Speedy's cage would go and who would get to take him home for the weekends.

The next e-mail was from Hannah,

who was Ella's best friend.

Dear Ella,

Thank you for the scarf you sent me from Peru. The colors are so pretty! I have a present I've been saving for you. I made it myself! Will you be home soon? I can give it to you then. It's snowing here. Is it snowing wherever you are?

Hugs,

Hannah

It's definitely snowing, Ella thought, peering out the window. At least a foot of new snow covered the city, and more continued to fall. For some

reason, it made her sad. If she were in Brookeston, she and Hannah would be ice-skating on Goose Pond or sledding down Hickory Hill.

"Hannah wants to know when we're coming home," Ella said to Ethan.

Ethan shrugged. "Probably never."

"I like our family trip. But I miss home," Ella said.

"Me too," agreed Ethan.

Just then, another e-mail popped up on the screen. It was from Grandpa Harry!

The twins sat up and began reading together.

TO: ethanella@eemail.com
FROM: gpaharry@eemail.com
SUBJECT: POLAR BEARS AND MORE!

Hello, my dears. Welcome to Alaska!

A little bird told me that you've been feeling homesick. When I was an archaeologist, I traveled all over the world to dig up ancient artifacts. I got homesick often.

Still, my trips were filled with so many adventures! I had some great ones when I was in Alaska. We dug up tools that were ten thousand years old—and mammoth tusks, too!

After the dig was over, I kayaked in Glacier Bay and I saw the northern lights in the night sky.

I also ran across a family of polar bears! The mother was feeding her two cubs.

Love,

Grandpa Harry

"How did Grandpa Harry know we were homesick?" Ella asked Ethan.

"He said a 'little bird' told him. What little bird?" said Ethan.

Ella shrugged and peered out the window again. The snow had stopped, and hundreds of stars twinkled in the sky. "The northern lights sound cool," she murmured.

"Glacier Bay must have lots of glaciers in it!" said Ethan.

"Do you think we'll see any polar bears?" Ella asked.

"Maybe we'll find a really old mammoth tusk!" Ethan said excitedly.

Ethan came over and joined his sister. Suddenly, the twins didn't feel quite so homesick anymore.

CHAPTER 3
Lost in the Wilderness

On Monday morning, the Briars flew from Anchorage to a city called Nome. Nome was on the coast of the Bering Sea. The sky was eerily dark during their flight. In this part of the world, the sun didn't rise until almost noon during the winter.

At the Nome Airport, they picked up their rental car. "Northward ho!"

Mr. Briar said as he drove out of the parking lot.

"What does that mean, Dad?" Ethan asked.

"It means we're heading north," Mr. Briar replied. "If you want our exact itinerary, your mother has that. Don't you, Jo?"

"Yes, I do!" Mrs. Briar reached into her purse and pulled out a small note-pad. She flipped to the first page. "For the next few days, we'll be traveling around the Seward Peninsula area—"

"'Peninsula' comes from the Latin words for 'almost island,'" Mr. Briar

cut in. "Hey, there's an idea! Maybe we should add Latin to our home-schooling lessons."

"No!" the twins said at the same time. They were busy enough with math, science, and all their other subjects.

"Anyway, we'll drive around the almost island and make some stops along the way." Mrs. Briar went on. "We'll visit an Alaska Native village. We'll check out a ghost town. We'll pan for gold at the beach."

"Awesome!" said Ethan.

They continued driving. Outside of
Nome, the scenery was beautiful and

wild. A herd of reindeer ran across
a snow-covered field. Mountains
loomed in the distance.

After a while, the road narrowed and led to a dense forest. Icicles dripped from tree branches. Snow began to fall—at first lightly, then more heavily.

Mr. Briar stopped the car and pulled out a map. "This doesn't look right. Did I miss my turn back there?"

"It's hard to see the road with all this snow," Mrs. Briar said anxiously.

Mr. Briar pointed. "I think it's *this* way." He turned the key in the ignition. The car sputtered and coughed. He tried again. The car sputtered and coughed again.

"Uh-oh. Bad news, gang. I think there's something wrong with our engine," Mr. Briar announced.

"But we're in the middle of nowhere!" Ella exclaimed.

Mrs. Briar frowned at her phone. "And there's no reception out here."

The snow was coming down faster now. The trees looked like blurry shadows.

"Maybe we should start walking," Ethan suggested. "We

could make snowshoes out of sticks
and rope!"

"We can't leave the car. We have no
idea where we are. Also, there could
be wild animals out there," Mr. Briar
pointed out.

"W-wild animals?" Ella stammered.

"Cool! I want to see a reindeer up
close," said Ethan.

Just then, Ella noticed something moving swiftly through the forest. It was coming closer and closer to their car. What was it?

Ella jabbed Ethan with her elbow. "Do you see that?" she whispered.

Ethan pressed his face against the cold glass. "Yeah. And I don't think it's a reindeer."

Suddenly, the *thing* was right next to their car. The twins gasped in surprise.

It was a dogsled . . . pulled by six huskies!

The dogs skidded to a stop, kicking up a powdery cloud of snow. A woman and a young girl stepped off the sled. They wore parkas with furry hoods and thick mittens.

"Help has arrived!" Mr. Briar cheered.

He and Mrs. Briar got out of the car. The twins got out, too.

"Hello there!" Mr. Briar called out to

GFS 009

the woman and the girl. "We've had some engine trouble. Do you know if there's an auto-repair shop nearby?"

"I'm afraid the nearest one is about fifty miles away," the woman replied.

Mrs. Briar raised her eyebrows. *"Fifty miles away?"*

The girl tugged on her mother's sleeve and whispered something in her ear.

"My daughter has a good idea," the woman said. "Why don't you come back to our village with us? We own a little inn. You could stay there until your car is fixed. A mechanic should be able to get here in two or three days."

Mr. Briar glanced at Mrs. Briar. She nodded.

"That's very kind. Thank you," Mrs. Briar said to the woman. "Wait—did you say two or three days?"

"It's the only auto-repair shop in this part of the state," the woman explained. "Also, it's not a quick trip. Most folks travel by sled or snow machine. But we'll take care of you until your car is fixed," she reassured the Briars.

The twins tried to hide their dis-
appointment. Waiting around for a
mechanic didn't sound nearly as fun
as visiting a ghost town or panning
for gold!

CHAPTER 4

The Fish Thief

The woman, Anna, and her daughter, Malina, took the Briars to their village by sled. It took two trips to get everyone there because the sled could fit only four people.

The village was tiny, with a few dozen houses, a general store, and a small school. Smoke curled out of chimneys. Snow gleamed in the fading light.

It was almost dark by the time everyone was settled in the living room of the Bear River Inn. A roaring fire crackled in the stone fireplace.

Anna showed the Briars to their

rooms. Mr. and Mrs. Briar had a large room with a view of the half-frozen Bear River and the woods. The twins had connecting rooms with animal themes. Ethan's had a hawk theme. Ella's had a walrus theme.

"My room and Malina's room are down the hall, if you need anything.

Oh, and our neighbors, George and Nolee Gardner, have invited us for dinner. Would you like to join us?" Anna asked.

"We'd love to!" Mrs. Briar answered for her family.

A short while later, the Briars followed Anna and Malina to the Gardners' house, which was right next door to the inn. It had stopped snowing, and the night sky glittered with stars. The icy ground crunched under their feet.

Ella pointed to a cluster of stars. "Are those the northern lights?" she

asked Malina, curiously.

Malina shook her head. "No. That's a constellation called Ursa Minor. That's Latin for 'Little Bear.' The northern lights are big, colorful lights

that flash across the sky. You can see them from here sometimes."

The group reached the Gardners' front porch. They heard loud voices from out back.

"They're gone!" someone cried out.

Anna, Malina, and the Briars rushed toward the back of the house. A man and a woman stood over a cooler. It was empty, and a faint fishy smell wafted up from it.

"George, Nolee, what's wrong?" Anna asked quickly.

Nolee threw up her hands. "The fish thief has taken our dinner!"

CHAPTER 5

A New Mystery

"The fish thief?" Ethan repeated.

"Yes, someone's been stealing fish from the folks in our village," Anna explained.

"It's quite the mystery," Nolee added.

Mystery! Ethan and Ella *loved* a good mystery. They'd cracked cases in a bunch of places around the world.

They'd even solved one in their own hometown!

"When was the last time you saw your fish?" Ella asked.

"Maybe an hour or two ago," replied George. "I just got back from an ice-fishing trip, and I stored my catch in this cooler."

"Last week the thief stole

fish from Hank Soto's cooler. And the week before, the thief stole fish from the Egans," Anna added.

"Luckily, I made other dishes. Why don't you all come in from the cold and we can eat," said Nolee.

Inside, everyone sat down at a long table while Nolee set out platters of food. She served roast potatoes and bread . . . and a strange-looking salad.

"The bread is called bannock. It's baked with blueberries and blackberries. The salad has fish eggs and

seaweed in it," Nolee told the Briars.

Mr. Briar beamed. "Fish eggs and seaweed? That sounds delicious!"

Ella tried a small bite of the salad to be polite. It actually wasn't so bad. As she ate, she wondered about all the

missing fish. Unless they swam out of the coolers on their own, *someone* must have taken them.

The question was who? And why?

Ethan nudged her. "I think you and I should try to catch this fish thief,"

he whispered through a mouthful of
bread.

Ella grinned. "I was just thinking
the same thing!"

They shook hands under the table.

* * *

The next day the twins asked their parents if they could go outside and build a snowman. But they didn't actually want to build a snowman. They wanted to search for clues in George and Nolee's yard, near where the cooler had been.

"Make sure you bundle up. It's cold out there!" Mrs. Briar called.

"My travel thermometer said it's minus-seven degrees Celsius. That's the same as nineteen degrees Fahrenheit!" Mr. Briar added.

Ella and Ethan put on their winter gear and hurried out the back door. They waved to the sled dogs, who lived in little wooden houses on stilts.

The twins walked to the edge of the

yard that bordered the Gardners' property. There was no car in their garage, and the windows of the house were dark. They quickly crossed into the Gardners' yard. It was easy, since there was no fence.

The cooler sat in the same spot as yesterday. Ella bent down and opened it. It was still empty and fishy-smelling.

Ethan knelt down next to Ella. He checked out the ground next to the cooler.

"Hey! Look!" he exclaimed, pointing.

Ella glanced over. There was a faint paw print in the snow!

CHAPTER 6
A Trail of Clues

The twins studied the icy paw print. It had five round toes like grapes.

Then Ethan noticed another paw print . . . and another. Some were identical to the first one. Others were *almost* identical.

"There's a whole bunch of them!" Ethan remarked.

"You're right!" said Ella.

"Check out the pattern. I bet it's a four-legged animal."

"Yes! These must be the front paws, and the other ones must be the back paws."

They followed the trail of paw prints across the Gardners' yard. The prints disappeared at the edge of the woods.

"They could be dog paw prints. Do you think one of Anna's sled dogs stole the fish?" Ethan asked.

"Maybe," Ella replied.

She reached into her parka for the special purple notebook that Grandpa Harry had given her. She pulled off one glove and flipped to a clean page.

Ethan peered over her shoulder. "What are you doing?"

"I'm going to draw our clues," Ella replied.

Ella found a pen in her pocket and quickly sketched a pair of paw prints, front and back.

"Okay. What's our next move?" asked Ethan.

"We should go visit the sled dogs and compare paw prints," Ella suggested.

The twins crossed back over to the other yard and went up to one of the doghouses. A husky poked its head out and thumped its tail.

Ella pet it. Its coat was thick and soft. "We're here to inspect your paw prints," she told the dog.

The dog thumped its tail again. Ethan crouched down next to Ella and surveyed the ground. "There are paw prints all over the place!"

Ella opened her notebook to the page with the paw prints she had just sketched. She and Ethan compared them to the paw prints on the ground.

"The dog paw prints have *four* toes. Our paw prints have *five*," said Ella.

She drew some quick pictures of the dog paw prints just in case. Then the twins went inside to warm up in front of the fireplace.

Malina was reading a book on the couch. She glanced up with a smile. "Hi! If you're looking for your parents, they're in the dining room with my mom."

"Thanks! Hey, Malina? Do you
know anything about paw prints?"
Ethan asked.

"Paw prints? I guess so. Why?" she answered.

Ethan and Ella told Malina about their case.

"We're trying to figure out who stole the fish from the cooler. We think it was an animal," Ella finished. She showed Malina her drawings of the mystery paw prints.

Malina jumped to her feet. "I think I can help you with this!"

CHAPTER 7
The Old Sketchbook

Malina went over to a bookshelf. She picked up a notebook with a leather cover.

"This is one of my grandma's sketchbooks. She was an artist," Malina explained. "She traveled all around Alaska and drew things from nature. Like plants, insects, animals . . . and animal tracks, too!"

Animal tracks! The twins grinned at each other.

Ethan noticed that the cover of the journal had a bird on it. And it looked a lot like the bird on the gold coin Grandpa Harry had given him. Ethan went to reach for the coin in his pocket, but Malina opened the sketchbook and began leafing through it.

The pages looked old and fragile. They were filled with drawings, and each drawing had a handwritten label.

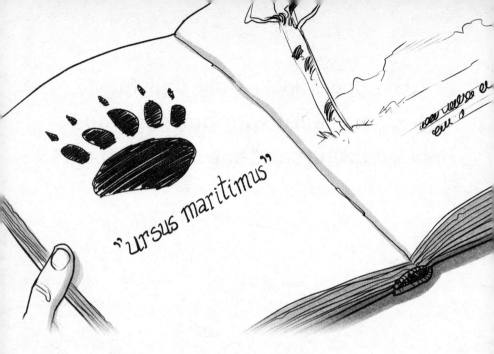

"ursus maritimus"

"Here." Malina stopped on a page with animal tracks on it.

Ella compared her own drawings to Malina's grandmother's drawings.

"Look!" Ella pointed to a set of animal tracks. "These are the same paw prints we saw!"

"That's weird. It says that these tracks belong to an *Ursus maritimus*," Malina said with a frown.

"Huh? What's an *Ur-sus mar-i-ti-mus*?" asked Ethan.

"Grandma always labeled her drawings in Latin. *'Ursus maritimus'* means 'polar bear.'"

Polar bear?

"So . . . a polar bear stole George and Nolee's fish?" Ella said.

Malina shook her head. "No way. There are no polar bears around here. We're too far south."

"How about a different kind of bear, then? Like a black bear or a brown bear?" Ethan suggested.

Malina turned to another page. "These are black bear tracks," she said, pointing. "And these are brown bear tracks. They look different from the polar bear ones." She added, "I remember my grandma saying that polar bears have way bigger paws than other kinds of bears. Their paws act like snowshoes and keep them

Black Bear front paw

Black Bear
rear paw

from slipping on ice and snow."

"Cool!" Ethan said. Ella nodded. They sure were learning a lot of interesting stuff on their trip around the world!

"So if the fish thief isn't a polar bear, a black bear, or a brown bear, then what is it?" asked Ella.

"I think I know how to find out," Ethan said mysteriously.

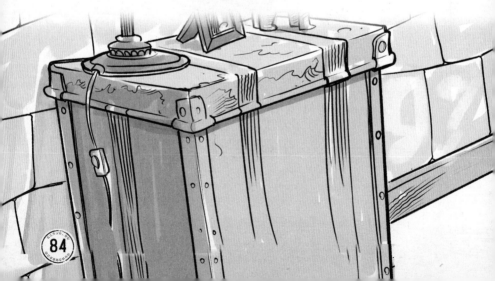

CHAPTER 8

The Fish Trap

Ethan, Ella, and Malina hurried into the dining room.

The three parents sat at the table drinking coffee. "Hey, kids! I just got off the phone with the mechanic. He'll be here the day after tomorrow to fix our car," said Mr. Briar.

"Until then, we can have a mini-holiday here. I'm going to

interview Anna for my article!" said
Mrs. Briar.

"It's very kind of your mother. She
thinks it will help attract lots of visi-
tors to the inn," Anna said, smiling at
Mrs. Briar.

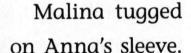

Malina tugged
on Anna's sleeve.
"Mama, may
we have some
fish?"

Anna looked
amused.
"Honey, if you
guys want a

snack, there's bread and cheese."

Ella spoke up. "But we're setting a trap for the fish thief. We think it's an animal!"

"How did you detectives come up with that theory?" asked Mr. Briar.

Ethan explained about finding the trail of paw prints. "Our plan is to put a cooler full of fish outside. Then we'll

wait for the thief to come back and try to steal again," he added.

Mrs. Briar frowned. "Wait a second. I thought you guys were building a snowman just now—not chasing thieves."

Ethan and Ella stared at each other.

"Um,"Ethan mumbled.

"Um," Ella mumbled.

Mr. Briar whispered

something to Mrs. Briar. Mrs. Briar whispered something to Anna.

"All right. If you guys want to try this plan, you have our permission," Mrs. Briar said after a moment. "It's not safe for you to be hanging out in the yard waiting for some wild animal to show up, though. Once you set the trap,

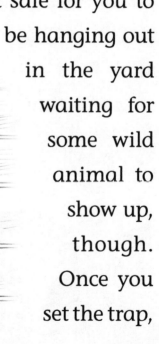

I want you to stay here and watch through a window."

"You can borrow my binoculars," Mr. Briar offered.

"I'll get the cooler and the fish," Anna said.

Ethan, Ella, and Malina exchanged high fives.

It was time to catch the fish thief!

* * *

"Do you see anything yet?" Ella whispered to Ethan.

Ethan squinted through the binoculars. "Nope. Not yet. And you've asked, like, a hundred times already!"

The twins and Malina had been keeping watch at the kitchen window all afternoon, waiting for someone— or something—to show up. They had placed the cooler of fish near the edge of the woods.

Malina glanced up at the sky. "It's almost nighttime. Maybe we should give up for today." Ethan

leaned toward the window. "Wait! I think see something!"

"What is it?" Ella grabbed the binoculars from him. She adjusted the knob to focus them.

Ethan was right! An animal hovered near the edge of the woods. It began moving toward the cooler.

"What is it? What is it?" Malina cried out.

"It's too dark to tell," replied Ella.

Just then, a *second* animal came bounding toward the first one.

"We have *two* fish thieves!" Ella announced.

CHAPTER 9

Closing In

Malina got a flashlight and flung open the back door. She clicked on the light and pointed it at the animals.

They startled and scurried into the woods.

"I'm sorry. They got away!" Malina apologized.

"Did anyone get a good look? Were they bears?" Ethan asked.

"I'm not sure," Ella replied.

"Me neither," said Malina.

"We can't follow them. Let's wait until tomorrow morning and try again," Ethan suggested, and the girls agreed.

* * *

The next day, the three kids headed outside right after sunrise. They went over to where the cooler sat in the snow.

Ethan opened the cooler. It was empty!

"Those animals must have returned in the middle of the night," Malina guessed.

"Look!" Ella said, pointing. The bear paw prints from the Gardners' yard dotted the snow.

Then she noticed a second set of paw prints. They had four toes instead of five. Ella tried to recall where she had seen them before. And then she remembered.

"These look just like the sled dogs' paw

prints, but they're even smaller," she said to Ethan and Malina.

"Peach!" Malina burst out.

"Peach, like the fruit?" asked Ethan.

"No! Peach is our new sled dog puppy. We adopted her a couple of months ago. These might belong to her!"

"So . . . Peach is one of the fish thieves?" Ella asked.

"Maybe. But who do the other paw prints belong to?" Malina wondered.

The three of them decided to put more fish in the cooler and repeat yesterday's stakeout. They also moved

the cooler closer to the back door. Then they took their positions in the kitchen.

It didn't take very long. After a few minutes, an animal lumbered out of the woods. It approached the cooler.

The creature was furry. And white.

Ella gasped. "Is that a . . . baby polar bear?"

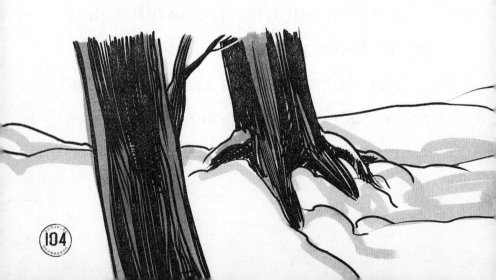

CHAPTER 10

Home Again

Malina gulped and nodded. "W-what's it doing here? It must be really far from its home!"

The polar bear cub pawed at the cooler. Just then, Peach burst out of her doghouse and bounded up to the cub. The two animals began tussling in the snow.

The cub got up and pawed at the

cooler again. Peach came over to help. The two animals knocked the cooler on its side, and the fish spilled out onto the icy ground.

Peach hung back as the cub gobbled up the fish. Then they resumed their playing. Peach slipped and skidded on the ice. The cub squealed happily. The two animals touched noses.

"They're talking with their noses!" Malina gushed. *"Awww!"*

"Awww!" Ella and Ethan joined in.

Now all they had to do was get the cub back to its *real* home!

The next day, the twins wrote an e-mail to Grandpa Harry:

Dear Grandpa Harry,

Guess what? We rescued a polar bear cub! We named him Marshmallow!

Marshmallow had been taking fish from the people in the village. The lady we're staying with called the animal-rescue people. They said Marshmallow got separated from his family and wandered south. He was hungry, which is why he took the fish.

The animal-rescue people took Marshmallow

back to his home. Marshmallow was sad to leave his new friend Peach. They touched noses goodbye. It's too bad polar bears and dogs can't e-mail each other like we can!

Still, Marshmallow must be happy to be with his family again. He seemed pretty homesick.

Love,

Ethan and Ella

PS By the way, we saw the northern lights last night! They were awesome!

Ethan Briar stared wide-eyed at the creepy statue. It stared back at him in the dim light of the underground corridor.

"Um, guys? What's that?" Ethan asked nervously.

His twin sister, Ella, giggled when she saw it. "I'm not sure. And is it supposed to be a person or an animal?"

"Both!" their father, Andrew Briar, spoke up. "This is Pan, one of the Greek gods. He's part human and part goat."

"Isn't he fascinating?" their mother, Josephine Briar, said excitedly. "Dr.

Pappas said they've already dug up ten statues at this site. So far, they're all figures from Greek mythology, like Pan."

The Briars had just arrived at an archaeological dig in Athens, Greece. Dr. Pappas was in charge of the site, which was more than two thousand years old! As an archaeologist, she was an expert in artwork, weapons, and other items left behind by people from the past.

Mrs. Briar had gotten special permission for herself and Mr. Briar to help out with the excavation. She was a travel writer, and she planned to write an article about it. Mr. Briar was a history professor back home.

"Back home" was a town called Brookeston in the United States. The Briars had been traveling around the world for many months now for Mrs. Briar's job. The Brookeston Times had hired her to write a column called "Journeys with Jo!" It was all about the different places their family was visiting, like France, India, Peru, Australia, Alaska—and now Greece!

"Can you guys find something to do for a while? Your dad and I need to check in with Dr. Pappas and get to work," Mrs. Briar said to the twins.

"Why can't we dig with you?" Ella asked.

"Yeah. We want to see what Grandpa Harry used to do!" Ethan added. Their Grandpa Harry was a famous archaeologist.

"Sorry, kids. This project is for adults only," Mr. Briar told them. "Say, why don't you go outside and find a nice, sunny place to hang out? You could do the reading for our Greek history lesson. You brought your books with you, right?"

The twins groaned. Homework was the last thing they felt like doing today. Besides, who needed books when real history was all around them?

Mr. and Mrs. Briar said good-bye and went off to join Dr. Pappas, who was brushing dirt from a clay figurine. Ethan and Ella began walking down the corridor. They passed a group of volunteers digging with small shovels. Everyone was wearing hard hats with headlamps, including the twins.

"How do we get up to the ground level?" Ella asked Ethan.

"We need to take the stairs. They're

that way," Ethan said, pointing to the right.

They walked on in silence. More corridors sprouted off in various directions. Electric lamps hung from wires and cast yellow pools of light. No one seemed to be working in this part of the site.

"Maybe we went the wrong way," Ella said anxiously.

"Ella! Look!"

Ethan stopped in front of a stone wall. On it was a painted image of a hawk. Next to the hawk was an image of a globe.

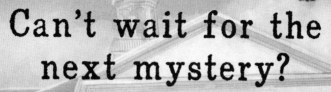